TEST OF TIME

Publisher's Cataloging in Publication Data

Crux. Volume two : test of time / Writer: Mark Waid ; Penciler: Steve Epting ; Inker: Rick Magyar ; Colorist: Frank D'Armata.

p. : ill. ; cm.

Spine title: Crux. 2 : test of time

ISBN 1-931484-36-8

1. Science fiction. 2. Adventure fiction. 3. Graphic novels. 4. Capricia (Fictitious character) 5. Tug (Fictitious character) 6. Zephyre (Fictitious character) 7. Galvan (Fictitious character) 8. Gammid (Fictitious character) 9. Verityn (Fictitious character) I. Waid, Mark. II. Epting, Steve. III. Magyar, Rick. IV. D'Armata, Frank. V. Title: Test of Time VI. Title: Crux. 2 : test of time.

PN6728 .C78 2002
813.54 [Fic]

CRUX®

TEST OF TIME

Mark **WAID**
W R I T E R

Steve **EPTING**
P E N C I L E R

Rick **MAGYAR**
I N K E R

Frank **D'ARMATA**
C O L O R I S T

CHAPTER II

Andy **SMITH** · PENCILER
Mark **FARMER** · INKER
Jeromy **COX** · COLORIST

Dave **LANPHEAR** · LETTERER

CrossGeneration Comics   **Oldsmar, Florida**

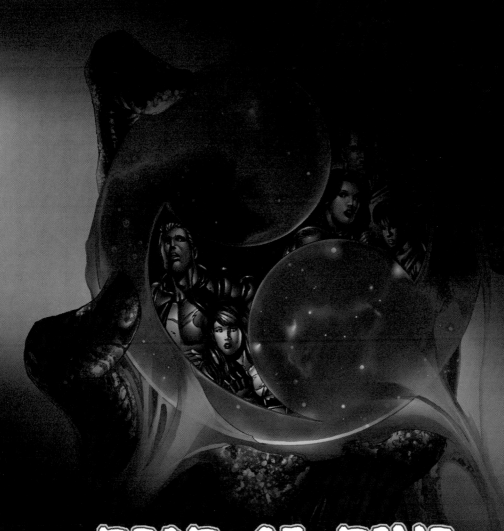

TEST OF TIME

features Chapters 7 - 12
of the ongoing series
CRUX

CR
STORY

THEY WERE THE ATLANTEANS, a peaceful civilization of artists and philosophers who used their phenomenal mental and physical skills to build an island utopia. They had but one responsibility: to guide and shepherd Earth's newborn race of *homosapiens* towards a grand and glorious destiny. But when a mysterious cataclysm plunged Atlantis and its people beneath the waves, six - and only six - were awakened by a mysterious stranger one thousand centuries later to find their utopia forgotten and in ruins,

U·X
So Far

their brothers and sisters caught in an unshakeable slumber... and the human race gone, having vanished centuries ago under mysterious circumstances.

Leading her group into mystery after mystery with no solutions in sight, Capricia's natural intensity and burden of responsibility backfired in the form of a brief but wild breakdown - crippling the team's ability to trust her. Now, having jeopardized the mutual bonds that are their only hope of survival, she must restore that trust...and quickly...

WITH A CONCENTRATION I COULD NEVER ATTEMPT IN *BATTLE*, I GET TO *WORK*.

AROUND THE CORNER, THE *OTHERS* CONTINUE TO SQUABBLE AND BICKER. THREATS ARE EXCHANGED.

THESE PEOPLE AREN'T *FRIENDS*. MANY OF THEM DIDN'T EVEN *KNOW* ONE ANOTHER BACK IN ATLANTIS. ALL THAT TIES THEM *TOGETHER* ARE A COMMON *HERITAGE* AND, FOR THE *MOST* PART...

...COMMON BELIEFS.

YOU'RE *JOKING*. THIS ISN'T THE *TIME* OR *PLACE*. AND WHERE DID YOU *GET*--

TWO: I *MADE* IT, AND *ONE:* YOU KNOW THE *RULES*.

IF *ONE* CALLS THE *CEREMONY*...

...ALL OTHERS *MUST* PARTICIPATE.

LET'S GET *PREPARED*.

CEREMONY?

YOU KNOW HOW I'VE SAID ALL ALONG WE WERE PHILOSOPHERS AND POETS MORE THAN WARRIORS? KEEP *WATCHING.*

THE *JATAKA TOTEM,* WHEN PRESENTED, BEGINS AN ATLANTEAN CEREMONY OF *BONDING.* PARTICIPANTS TAKE TURNS EXERCISING THEIR *IMAGINATION* BY CREATING *HISTORY.*

CRE--? BUT HISTORY IS THE ASSEMBLY OF *FACTS.*

IS IT? WHAT KILLED THE *DINOSAURS?* VOLCANIC *ERUPTIONS* OR A *METEOR* STRIKE? WHICH THEORY IS *CORRECT?*

WE DON'T *KNOW.* AT THIS POINT, ONE'S AS GOOD AS THE *OTHER,* I GUESS.

EXACTLY.

"GEROMI, THE *ATLANTEAN* SAGA GOES BACK *100 MILLION YEARS,* ALMOST *NONE* OF THEM *DOCUMENTED.*

"ANCIENT HISTORY IS WHATEVER OUR IMAGINATION *TELLS* US IT IS.

"IT'S WHATEVER STORY WE CARE TO *CREATE...* SO, USING THE *JATAKA* TO DESIGNATE *TURNS,* WE...*MAKE HISTORY,* IF YOU WILL. TOGETHER, WE CREATE A *STORY.*

"IT SOUNDS LIKE A *GAME,* BUT IT'S *NOT.* AS THE STORY *GROWS,* WE FIND IT TENDS TO TAKE ON A LIFE OF ITS *OWN.*

"SOMETIMES, ITS *CONCLUSION* SHEDS LIGHT ON THE OBSTACLES *BEFORE* US.

"OTHER TIMES, ITS *TELLING* REVEALS MUCH ABOUT THE *TELLER.*

"REGARDLESS..."

"...IT'S PROBABLY OUR *LAST HOPE.*

I WAS THINKING ABOUT THE *DINOSAURS* EARLIER...SO THAT'S WHERE THIS *STARTS.*

"WITH A *METEOR* THE SIZE OF A SMALL *MOON*...

"...STRIKING THE OCEAN WITH *UNIMAGINABLE FORCE*... SPEWING VAST GOUTS OF *STEAM* AND EXTRATERRESTRIAL *DUST* INTO THE *SKIES*...

"...AND ENSHROUDING THE EARTH IN *TOTAL DARKNESS.*

"IN A SPLIT-SECOND, A *VIOLENT ACTION* CHANGED *EVERYTHING.*"

"SICK AND TIRED OF LOSS, HE TRIED TO **BUILD** SOMETHING. HE WORKED TO BRING **UNITY** TO WARRING TRIBES, WARRING **NATIONS**...

"...AND **FAILED.**

"ALL HE REALLY HAD TO **OFFER** WAS A **DREAM**...AND IN THE FACE OF **REALITY**, THAT WAS LESS THAN **USELESS.**

THE PROBLEM **WAS**, A GOAL AS EPHEMERAL AS "PEACE" OR "HARMONY" WASN'T **MOTIVE** ENOUGH -- NOT WITH THE VERY **REAL** FEAR AND HARDSHIP HIS PEOPLE STILL FACED.

AND...

...AND THAT'S WHEN THOLAN **SAW** SOMETHING.

"A SOLDIER WEARING A BADGE **IDENTICAL** TO THE ONE ON THE DAGGER THAT KILLED THOLAN'S **WIFE.**

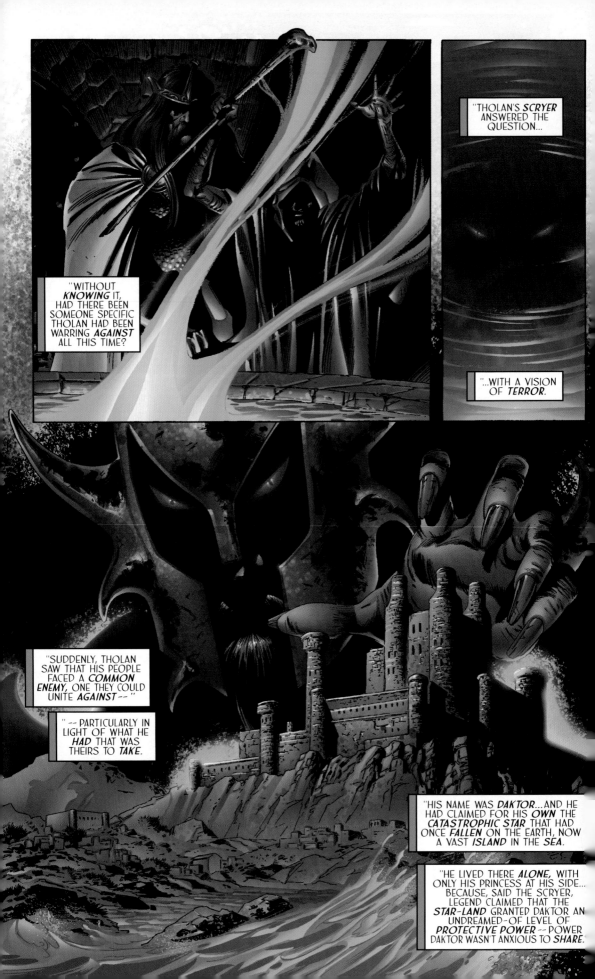

"THOLAN'S *SCRYER* ANSWERED THE QUESTION...

"WITHOUT *KNOWING* IT, HAD THERE BEEN SOMEONE SPECIFIC THOLAN HAD BEEN WARRING *AGAINST* ALL THIS TIME?"

"...WITH A VISION OF *TERROR*."

"SUDDENLY, THOLAN SAW THAT HIS PEOPLE FACED A *COMMON ENEMY,* ONE THEY COULD UNITE *AGAINST* --"

" -- PARTICULARLY IN LIGHT OF WHAT HE *HAD* THAT WAS THEIRS TO *TAKE.*

"HIS NAME WAS *DAKTOR*...AND HE HAD CLAIMED FOR HIS *OWN* THE *CATASTROPHIC STAR* THAT HAD ONCE *FALLEN* ON THE EARTH, NOW A VAST *ISLAND* IN THE *SEA.*

"HE LIVED THERE *ALONE,* WITH ONLY HIS PRINCESS AT HIS SIDE... BECAUSE, SAID THE SCRYER, LEGEND CLAIMED THAT THE *STAR-LAND* GRANTED DAKTOR AN *UNDREAMED-OF* LEVEL OF *PROTECTIVE POWER* -- POWER DAKTOR WASN'T ANXIOUS TO *SHARE.*

"THOLAN VOWED TO LEAD *HIS* PEOPLE *TO* THAT MYSTERIOUS POWER -- AND IN DOING SO, AVENGE HIS OWN WIFE'S *DEATH*.

"GUIDED BY *HIS VISION,* THEY SET OUT IN SEARCH OF THEIR *DESTINY.*"

"AT *FIRST*, THOLAN'S SOLDIERS WERE *GALVANIZED* BY HIS SHEER *DETERMINATION*.

"HE LET *NOTHING* STAND BETWEEN THEM AND THE POSSIBILITY OF *MAGICAL STRENGTH*.

"TO *THOLAN*, EVERY *HARDSHIP* ALONG THE *WAY* WAS PROOF THAT THEY WERE ON THE RIGHT *PATH*...

"...BUT IF THEY *WERE*, THEN WHY WAS THERE *TOLL* AFTER *TOLL?* EVERYTHING THAT CAME *AT* THEM, EVERY NEW OBSTACLE IN THEIR *WAY*, WAS HARDER TO OVERCOME THAN THE *LAST* AND COST *LIVES*.

"THERE WEREN'T EVEN ANY *VICTORIES*.

"JUST *SURVIVAL*."

"BUT THOLAN WOULDN'T LET HIS MEN *SURRENDER*.

"THEY SAILED SO LONG, SOMETIMES THEY FORGOT WHAT IT WAS--*WHO* IT WAS-- THEY WERE LOOKING *FOR*.

"AND YET, ON THEY *WENT*.

"EVENTUALLY, THEY WERE LEFT WITH NOTHING. THEY'D FOLLOWED A *FANATIC* AND REALIZED WHAT A HORRIBLE PRICE THEY'D PAID--

"--TOO *LATE*.

"AND STILL, THOLAN WOULDN'T LET THEM REST.

"HE *SWORE* DAKTOR'S LAND WAS IN *SIGHT*--THEIRS TO *CLAIM* --

"--BUT THEY'D BEEN DRIVEN TOO HARD FOR TOO *LONG* BY A MAN WHOSE *OBSESSION* CAUSED HIM TO LOSE SIGHT OF WHO HE WAS FIGHTING *FOR*.

"IN THE END, HIS MEN HAD NO CHOICE BUT TO *ABANDON* HIM...

...AND THEY WENT THEIR *OWN WAY.*

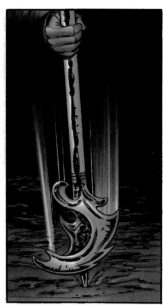

THERE'S *MORE.*

"BATTERED BY THE SEA, WEAKENED TO THE BRINK OF *DEATH,* THOLAN NEVERTHELESS SUBSISTED ON SHEER *DETERMINATION.*

"HE HAD *FOUND* DAKTOR'S ISLAND... AND HE CRAWLED *ASHORE...*

"...MORE READY THAN *EVER* TO DO *BATTLE.*

"ULTIMATELY, WHATEVER MAGIC MIGHT HAVE *SHIELDED* DAKTOR FROM THOLAN'S UNCOMPROMISING *QUEST*...WELL...

"...THAT'S THE *THING* ABOUT OBSESSION.

"IF IT'S STRONG ENOUGH... IT CUTS THROUGH *ANYTHING.*"

"STILL IN BATTLE-RAGE, THOLAN GRABBED DAKTOR'S PRINCESS BY THE THROAT--

"--AND HOLDING HER UP BEFORE HIS ENEMY, THREATENED TO KILL HER, *TOO*--

"--UNLESS DAKTOR USED HIS DYING BREATH TO EXPLAIN AND *SURRENDER* THE MAGIC CONFERRED BY THE VERY GROUND BENEATH THEIR *FEET*.

"AND DAKTOR...

"...DAKTOR *LAUGHED*.

"THAT MAGIC WAS A *MYTH*, HE CONFESSED. ONE PUT FORTH BY DAKTOR *HIMSELF* TO HELP SPIN A LEGEND OF *SUPREMACY*. THERE WAS NO POWER TO THE *LAND*.

"THOLAN HAD COME ALL THIS WAY FOR *NOTHING*. HE HAD LIED TO HIS *MEN* AND TO *HIMSELF*. ALL *ALONG*, HE'D BEEN WARNED THAT HIS QUEST WAS *AIMLESS*...

"...AND *FUTILE*."

"THE RAIN POURED ON THOLAN FOR DAYS BEFORE IT EVEN *OCCURRED* TO HIM TO BUILD A SHELTER FROM THE *STORM*.

"AND THAT'S WHEN HE *REALIZED* SOMETHING.

"DAKTOR WAS WRONG. THERE *WAS* POWER TO THE LAND.

"THOLAN HAD *FAILED* HIS FOLLOWERS BY LETTING HIS OWN PERSONAL *DEMONS* CHART THEIR COURSE... BUT IN THE END, HE HAD *LEARNED* SOMETHING.

"IF HE TRULY WANTED TO *LEAD*...

"...IF HE WANTED HIS PEOPLE TO *SURVIVE*...TO *THRIVE* IN THE HOSTILE WORLD AROUND THEM...

"...HE HAD TO PROVIDE SOMETHING *REAL* FOR THEM.

"NOT A *'MAGIC.'* NOT SOME VAGUE AND EPHEMERAL *'BETTER FUTURE'* THAT MIGHT SOMEHOW *'UNIFY'* MEN.

"SOMETHING *SOLID*...

"...AND WORTH WORKING *TOWARDS.*"

...TELLING ME YOU'RE *SURE* ABOUT THIS?

I RAN EVERYTHING YOU *ASKED* ME TO RUN, AND YOU WERE *RIGHT*.

WE ALL *MISSED* IT...WHICH I, FOR ONE, FIND *EXTRAORDINARILY* EMBARRASSING... BUT YOU WERE *RIGHT*.

THEN GET *READY*.

YOU'RE ON IN *FIVE*.

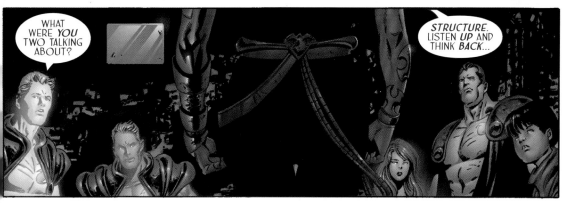

WHAT WERE *YOU* TWO TALKING ABOUT?

STRUCTURE. LISTEN *UP* AND THINK *BACK*...

...TO WHEN WE FIRST *MET* GEROMI. HE SAID SOMETHING THAT *ALL* OF US, IN OUR RATHER... *CONFUSED STATE,* LET SLIP RIGHT BY.

HE MADE A REFERENCE TO EARTH'S "*SIX CONTINENTS*"... BUT AT THE TIME ATLANTIS *SANK*...

ESTERDAY, SILENT RED AS NOWHERE TO BE EEN. THAT HE COMES ND GOES AS HE PLEASES DOESN'T BOTHER ME.

'S HOW HIS PRESENCE ENERALLY MAKES NO IFFERENCE. WORSE, GHT NOW, HE'S SETTING NEW RECORD FOR ASSIVITY.

I'D LABEL HIS EXPRESSION "CONFUSED" IF I THOUGHT HE WERE CAPABLE OF EMOTIONS.

LIKE GRIEF. THE TWINS...

WE ARE SO BADLY OUTNUMBERED.

IF I LURE SOME OF THESE CREATURES AWAY FROM TUG AND THE OTHERS, MAYBE IT'LL EVEN THE ODDS...

...AND KEEP US FROM DYING FOR ANOTHER FEW MINUTES.

--BUT--IMAGINE *THAT!*--
HE *STRANGER* NOT
ONLY *CAN* SAVE THEM--

--BUT PLAYING
COMPLETELY
AGAINST TYPE--

--HE *DOES!*

MAYBE WE *DON'T* DIE
TODAY. MAYBE *NOW* WE
CAN *FIGHT BACK* AND--

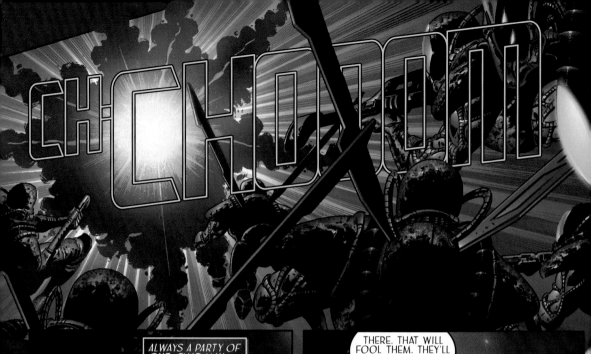

CH-CHO:OOM

ALWAYS A PARTY OF *ONE*, THAT MAN.

THERE. THAT WILL FOOL THEM. THEY'LL BELIEVE US *DEAD*... AT LEAST FOR *NOW*.

WHERE--?

A LITTLE *WARNING* NEXT TIME...

I'VE BEEN *TRYING* TO TELL YOU. THIS *"AUSTRALIA"* PLACE IS *STILL HERE*. IT'S JUST *CLOAKED* SOMEHOW!

THEN THE *TWINS*--

NO DOUBT HERE AS *WELL*. COME.

LET US *FIND* THEM BEFORE THE SOLDIERS ABOVE REALIZE THEY'VE BEEN *DECEIVED*...

...AND DECIDE TO *INVESTIGATE*.

...SO THAT'S WHERE THE *SMALLNESS* OF THE CAGE WORKS TO OUR *ADVANTAGE*. IF I POSITION MYSELF RIGHT, I CAN *BLOCK* WHILE YOU DO *YOUR* PART.

READY?

NO.

NO?

I DON'T LIKE THE *PLAN.*

IT'S *ALWAYS SOMETHING* WITH YOU, YOU *INGRATE!* WHAT'S SO *WRONG* WITH IT?

JUST ONE THING.

YOU MADE THE WRONG *BROTHER* THE *TARGET.*

GAMMID, *NO!*

DON'T *ARGUE! GO!*

AAAAGGH!

GO!

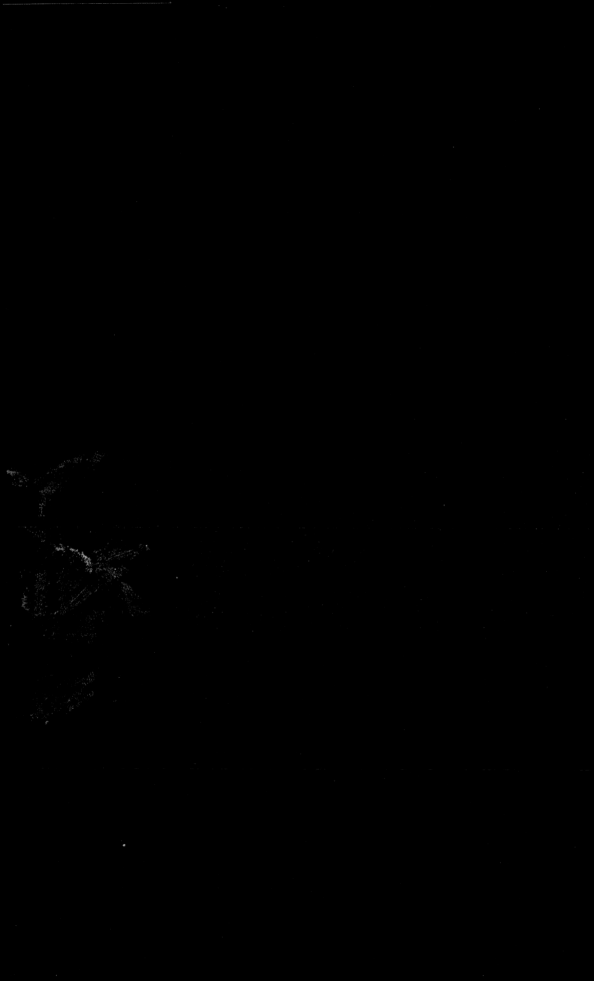

"...THE FIRST TIME, FOR EXAMPLE, WE WERE ALMOST *THERE*. CONSTRUCTION WAS *HOURS* FROM COMPLETION...

"...THE *MACHINE* ENGINEERED AROUND AN IRREPLACEABLE RADIOACTIVE *ORE* MINED FROM THE *NORTH CLIFFS* TWENTY YEARS *PREVIOUS*. WITHOUT THAT ORE, THE REST OF THE MACHINE WOULD BE *USELESS*...

"...SO, OF *COURSE*, JUST BEFORE WE COULD PUT IT TO *USE*...IT *VANISHED* FROM TECHNICIAN DRURAN'S HANDS.

"A SECOND LATER, DRURAN *HIMSELF* FELT A PRICKLING TINGLE OF ENERGY--

"--AND IN AN *EMERALD HAZE*, THE WORLD *AROUND* HIM FADED *FROM* HIS SIGHT--"

"-- REPLACED IN A *BLINK* BY AN ENTIRELY *NEW* -- AND *BAFFLING* -- POINT-OF-VIEW.

"DRURAN'S MIND WAS *REELING.* THE *ORE* FRAGMENT WAS THERE *WITH* HIM -- BUT HOW COULD THEY BE PULLING IT *FRESH* FROM A *MINE?* HADN'T THAT ALREADY *HAPPENED?*

"WAS HE *HALLUCINATING?* EXPERIENCING SOME WEIRD *VISION?*

"NO, NO, HE WAS THERE IN THE *FLESH* -- HIS SUDDEN PRESENCE *STARTLING* THE *MINER* --

"-- HIS PHYSICAL MASS *TEETERING* THE SCAFFOLD HANGING FROM THE *NORTH CLIFFS* --"

"--THE CASCADE OF HIS *ARRIVAL* TUMBLING THE MINER--AND THE *ORE*-- INTO *FREEFALL*--"

"--NEVER TO BE *RECOVERED*."

"DRURAN WAS *SPEECHLESS* WITH THE HORROR OF *REALIZATION*. WITHOUT INTENT -- WITHOUT *WARNING* -- HE HAD SOMEHOW BEEN PULLED THROUGH *TIME* --"

"--AND HAD IN AN *INSTANT* CHANGED *HISTORY*. HE HAD *DESTROYED* THE ORE BEFORE IT COULD EVER BE *USED*--MAKING MONTHS OF BUILDING AND CONSTRUCTION *POINTLESS*."

"IT WAS AN *ACCIDENT*-- BUT THE *SCAR* LEFT BY WHATEVER ENERGY HAD *TRANSPORTED* HIM NONETHELESS MARKED HIS *GUILT*."

"IN A *DAZE*, DRURAN WANDERED THE STREETS OF HIS *CHILDHOOD*. OCCASIONALLY, HE SAW *OTHERS* SCARRED *LIKE* HIM--COWERING, WITHDRAWN, *MOTIONLESS*."

"HE TRIED REACHING *OUT* TO THEM, BUT THEY WOULD NOT REACH *BACK*."

"A VICTIM OF FORCES *UNKNOWN*, DRURAN QUICKLY SANK INTO DESPAIR--"

"--BUT WHEN HE SAW *HIMSELF* AS A *YOUNG BOY*-- SO FULL OF *LIFE*, SO *UNAWARE* OF WHAT SADISM DESTINY HAD IN *STORE* FOR HIM--DRURAN *SNAPPED*.

"HE BEGAN *BADGERING* ONE OF THE *SCARRED*--DEMANDING SHE *SPEAK* TO HIM, *EXPLAIN* HERSELF, DO *SOMETHING*--

"--AND SHE *DID*. SHE FLED IN *TERROR*--

"--AS SHE RAN, KNOCKING *YOUNG* DRURAN OFF HIS *FEET*--

"--AND DIRECTLY INTO THE PATH OF AN APPROACHING *HOVERBIKE*.

"FRANTICALLY, *ADULT* DRURAN MOVED TO PULL THE BOY TO *SAFETY*--

"--TOO *LATE*."

"SUDDENLY, MEMORIES BEGAN TO *EXPLODE* IN DRURAN'S HEAD -- MEMORIES THAT, UNTIL THAT *SECOND,* HAD NEVER *EXISTED.*"

"IN THAT INSTANT, HE REMEMBERED NOT ONLY THE *TRAUMA* OF THAT COLLISION --"

"--BUT WHAT IT HAD *COST* HIM."

"DRURAN NOW UNDERSTOOD WHY THOSE *LIKE* HIM WERE SO *FRIGHTENED.* THEY, *TOO,* HAD BEEN FLUNG THROUGH TIME."

"THEY, *TOO,* HAD DISCOVERED THAT TO INTERACT WITH THE PAST, TO AFFECT IT IN ANY WAY--EVEN TO *SPEAK* THE WRONG *WORDS* --WOULD SET IN MOTION A CHAIN OF EVENTS THAT WOULD CHANGE THE *FUTURE.*"

"DRURAN WAS AMONG THE *FIRST* TO LEARN THIS. BY *NOW,* WE *ALL* HAVE. BY NOW, EVERY MAN, WOMAN AND CHILD IN THIS *LAND* HAS BEEN CATAPULTED *REPEATEDLY* THROUGH THE TIMESTREAM --"

"-- SOMETIMES TEN DAYS BACK, SOMETIMES TEN *CENTURIES*-- TOTALLY AT *RANDOM*--LEAVING THEM *PARALYZED,* AFRAID TO DO MUCH OF *ANYTHING* --"

"--FOR FEAR THEY'LL CREATE A CAUSALITY EFFECT THAT WILL REMOVE *THEMSELVES* FROM EXISTENCE."

-- SO I SENT AN INVESTIGATIVE TEAM.

GENTLEMEN, WELCOME TO EARTH'S *POWER SOURCE:* THE *TACHYON SUPERCOLLIDER.*

THE MAGNETS THAT CONTROL IT *ALONE* ARE STRONG ENOUGH TO WONK OUT THE *ELECTROMAGNETIC SPECTRUM* ALL OVER THE *CONTINENT* -- HENCE THE BIZARRE *COLOR* OF THE SKY. AND THAT'S NOT EVEN THE *IMPRESSIVE* PART.

WHAT'S *IMPRESSIVE* IS THAT THE SUPERCOLLIDER PROVIDES ENERGY *WORLDWIDE* --

-- DESPITE, I MIGHT ADD, THE FACT THAT IT'S CURRENTLY *LEAKING LIKE A SIEVE.*

AND *THAT* IS WHY THE *CALENDAR* BUSINESS IS SO DEPRESSED HERE IN *AUSTRALIA.*

SEE, *TACHYONS* ARE *FASTER-THAN-LIGHT PARTICLES* WITH -- THEY SAY -- *TIME-TRAVEL PROPERTIES.*

NO ONE'S EVER *PROVEN* THAT *LAST* PART, BUT GIVEN WHAT WE'VE *SEEN,* I'M GOING OUT ON A *LIMB* AND SAY, *YEAH, IT'S TRUE* --

-- ESPECIALLY IF THEY'RE ROCKETING *UNRESTRAINED* THROUGH THE AREA.

NO WONDER AUSTRALIA'S SUCH A MESS IF IT'S *GROUND ZERO.* TIME'S NOT FLOWING LINEARLY FOR MUCH OF *ANYTHING* --

-- INCLUDING *ROCKS,* BY THE WAY. YOU JUST *CONKED* YOUR PAST SELF IN THE *HEAD.*

PAK

STUPID *ROCK...*

OW!

CAPRICIA...

...THE GATE ITSELF IS MECHANICAL, TRUE... BUT NOT THE *YEARNING*.

WHAT HAVE WE *NOW?* SO MANY SO *FRIGHTENED* TO *LIVE* THAT I AND A FEW OTHERS FEEL *COMPELLED* TO MOVE US *BEYOND* THAT STATE *REGARDLESS* OF THE RISK.

I TAKE *RESPONSIBILITY* FOR MY PEOPLE. SURELY YOU CAN UNDERSTAND THAT.

I...

OF COURSE.

REALLY, CAPRICIA, WE'RE ON TOP OF IT. KNOWING WHAT WE KNOW *NOW,* ZEPH AND I HAVE TAKEN ALL *POSSIBLE* ENERGY-FEEDBACK INTO ACCOUNT IN WAYS *NO* ONE IN ATLANTIS DID.

WE TRULY BELIEVE WE'VE MADE THIS INTO A *RISK-FREE PROPOSITION.*

IF THAT WAS YOUR CONCERN, PLEASE PUT IT *ASIDE* AND PITCH *IN.* TRUE, YOUR UNEXPECTED PRESENCE HAS GREATLY ACCELERATED CONSTRUCTION...

...BUT THE LONGER YOU *STAY,* THE GREATER THE CHANCE SOMEONE FROM *YOUR* GROUP MIGHT ALSO BE SWEPT UP IN THE *TIME-JAUNT* ENERGY...WHICH HELPS *NO* ONE.

I TAKE *EVERYONE'S* WELFARE INTO ACCOUNT, CAPRICIA. *IF* THAT WAS YOUR CONCERN.

AND THERE THEY GO *ARM-IN-ARM* AGAIN. THEY SEEM TO KNOW WHAT THEY'RE *TALKING* ABOUT, THOSE TWO. IN FACT, THEY'VE GOTTEN ANNOYINGLY *FRIENDLY* ANNOYINGLY *FAST.*

IT IS THE QUESTION OF *SAFETY* THAT'S BOTHERING ME...

...ISN'T IT?

VERITYN...?

VERITYN!

THE STRANGER! WHY DID HE--?

HE KNEW IT WAS *TOO LATE*, ZEPHYRE.

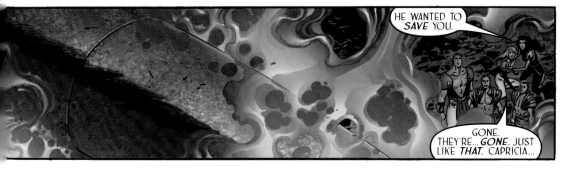

HE WANTED TO *SAVE* YOU.

GONE. THEY'RE... *GONE*. JUST LIKE *THAT*. CAPRICIA...

LADY SAMAKAR, THOSE *NOISES*--!

I THOUGHT THE *ATLANTEANS* WENT TO *REPAIR* OUR GENERATOR-- NOT *SABOTAGE* IT *FURTHER!* WHAT ARE THEY--?

I HAVE NO *IDEA*, AND FRANKLY, I DON'T *CARE*. WE'RE CLOSER TO ACHIEVING OUR *OWN* GOALS THAN *EVER*, AND WE HAVEN'T THE TIME TO *INVESTIGATE*.

ALL WE *CAN* DO IS CARRY ON WITH THE *CONSTRUCTION*--

--AND HOPE THEY'RE *ALL RIGHT*.

ALL *WRONG*. THIS IS *ALL WRONG*.

FIRST, THE STRANGER AND VERITYN *VANISH*--

--AND BEFORE WE CAN EVEN PROCESS *THAT*, WE'RE UNDER *ATTACK. AGAIN*.

BUT IT'S NOT *LIKE* THE OTHER TIMES. *BEFORE*, WE COULD AT LEAST STAND OUR *GROUND* AGAINST OUR NEGATION ASSAILANTS.

THIS *NEW* ONE IS USING WEAPONS THAT MAKE *THEIRS* LOOK LIKE *SLINGSHOTS*.

DON'T KNOW WHICH WAY THE OTHERS *RAN*, BUT AT LEAST I PUT SOME *DISTANCE* BETWEEN MYSELF AND THE *ENEMY*.

NOW AT LEAST I HAVE A CHANCE TO PLAN SOME SORT OF *COUNTERATTACK*.

I'M DEAD.

DEAD.

D—E

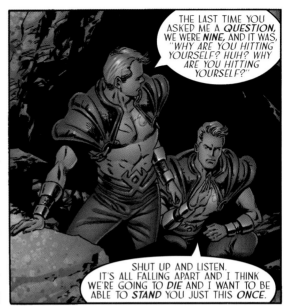

THE LAST TIME YOU ASKED ME A *QUESTION,* WE WERE *NINE,* AND IT WAS, "WHY ARE YOU HITTING YOURSELF? HUH? WHY ARE YOU HITTING YOURSELF?"

SHUT UP AND LISTEN. IT'S ALL FALLING APART AND I THINK WE'RE GOING TO *DIE* AND I WANT TO BE ABLE TO *STAND* YOU JUST THIS *ONCE.*

YOU CAN'T *STAND* ME. LITTLE *HARSH.*

JUST FIGURE SOMETHING *OUT,* OKAY? *HURRY!*

WHY IS THIS UP TO--

BECAUSE YOU'RE THE *SMART* ONE!

YOU'RE THE *SMART* ONE.

LOOK, I'M NOT--

AND DON'T *CONDESCEND.* YOU'RE ONLY MAKING IT *WORSE.* YOU'RE SO *ARROGANT*--!

SAYS THE *LOUDMOUTH*.

LOUDMOUTHS GET *HEARD*.

YOU REALLY CAN'T *STAND* ME.

LET'S NOT TALK ABOUT THIS ANY MORE.

WE NEED A *PLAN*, AND WE BOTH KNOW IT HAD BETTER NOT BE *MINE*, BECAUSE MINE ALWAYS INVOLVES LEADING WITH OUR *FACES*.

OKAY. GEROMI SAID THE REASON WE'RE HAVING TROUBLE ACCESSING *EM* ENERGY IS BECAUSE OF THE MAGNET IN THAT STUPID *SUPERCOLLIDER*, CORRECT? IT'S WARPING THE WHOLE *SPECTRUM* HERE, RIGHT?

WELL, I REFUSE TO HAVE MY CAUSE OF DEATH BE A *MAGNET*. WE HAVEN'T *POOLED* OUR POWER FOR A WHILE NOW --

-- AND WHILE THE *WHY* OF THAT IS *ABUNDANTLY* CLEAR, WE HAVE *GOT* TO WORK *TOGETHER*. BETWEEN THE *TWO* OF US, WE OUGHT TO BE ABLE TO MANAGE *SOMETHING* IN THE WAY OF FIREPOWER.

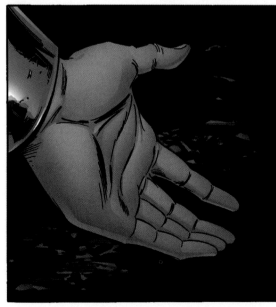

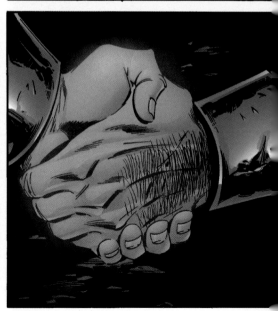

IT **WORKED.** EXPLODING THE DEVICE THE HUNTER WAS USING TO DRAW ENERGY FROM HIS **HOME DIMENSION** TOOK HIM OUT. **HARD.**

BEFORE I CAN GET **TWO WORDS** OUT OF MY MOUTH, ZEPH HAS STRIPPED OUR UNCONSCIOUS CAPTIVES OF THEIR **WEAPONS** AND BOUND THEM WITH SCRAP CABLE FROM THE **SUPERCOLLIDER.**

THIS IS A **NEW EXPERIENCE** FOR US. FINALLY, WE'VE CAPTURED SOMEONE WHO--ONCE THEY WAKE **UP**--CAN **TELL** US SOMETHING ABOUT THIS "**NEGATION**" THAT SO BADLY WANTS US **DEAD. INVALUABLE** INFORMATION.

FIRST, THOUGH, WE'VE GOT TO **FINISH** WHAT WE CAME HERE TO **DO.** THE AUSTRALIANS ARE **COUNTING** ON US... AND COUNTING THE **MINUTES** WE'RE **GONE.**

WITH GEROMI'S DIRECTIONS AND HELP FROM TUG'S TK, ZEPH HURRIES TO PATCH UP THE **SUPERCOLLIDER,** STAVING OFF--HOWEVER **TEMPORARILY**--THE **CHRONAL DISCHARGES** THAT HAVE **PLAGUED** THE LOCALS...

...WHILE THE TWINS HEAD BACK TO ADVISE **SAMAKAR.**

GAMMID, LOOK-- ABOUT WHAT I-- WHAT I **SAID** BEFORE--

NO, I'M GLAD YOU SPOKE YOUR **MIND.** WE'VE **BOTH** BEEN HOLDING BACK **TOO LONG,** AND THE TRUTH **IS**--

--I CAN'T STAND YOU, **EITHER.**

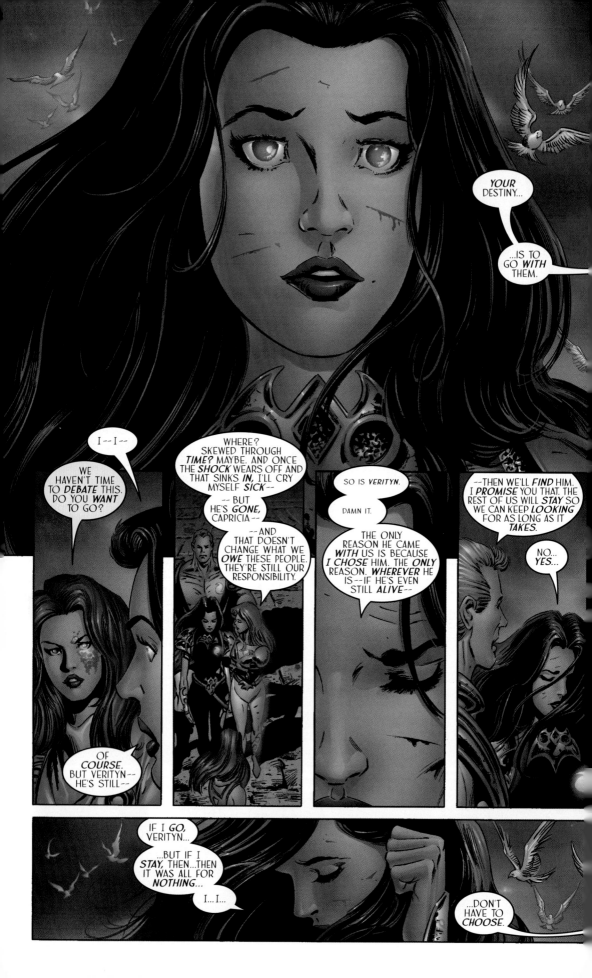

I'LL GO.

GAMMID? NO. YOU CAN'T--

WHAT'S THE *ALTERNATIVE?* SPENDING THE REST OF MY LIFE WATCHING YOU *TORTURE* YOURSELF OVER THIS? NO.

YOU'RE RIGHT. WE CAN'T LEAVE VERITYN *BEHIND.* BUT *TUG* IS RIGHT, TOO. *SOMEONE* SHOULD SHEPHERD HUMANITY...GO FIND ANSWERS TO ALL THE QUESTIONS THAT... THAT *ARE.* WHY *NOT* ME?

DON'T BE AN *ASS.*

WHAT, SUDDENLY IT'S *YOUR* TURN TO BE THE *SHOWOFF?*

AS HARD AS THIS MAY BE FOR YOU TO *BELIEVE,* THIS ISN'T ABOUT *YOU,* NOR IS IT ABOUT SHOWING YOU *UP.*

WE BOTH KNOW THIS IS FOR THE *BEST.*

AND DON'T PRETEND TO BE *INDIGNANT.* WE MAY BE *BROTHERS,* GALVAN, BUT WE HAVE *NEVER* BEEN FRIENDS, AND THE WAY YOU *TREAT* ME...

...I DON'T THINK WE EVER *WILL* BE.

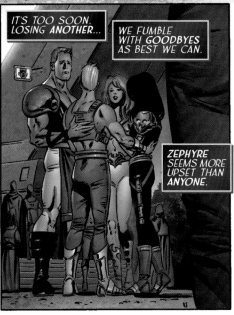

IT'S TOO SOON. LOSING *ANOTHER...*

WE FUMBLE WITH *GOODBYES* AS BEST WE CAN.

ZEPHYRE SEEMS MORE UPSET THAN *ANYONE.*

THAN *ANYONE.*

EVERY **MINUTE** OF EVERY **DAY** IS A **CHOICE**.

LEFT/RIGHT. THINK/ACT. KIND/CRUEL.

IN THIS UNIVERSE, THERE ARE FORCES BEYOND ALL COMPREHENSION BEARING RELENTLESSLY UPON US, TRYING TO STEER US OR SHAPE US, SOMETIMES SUCCEEDING...ON THE **OUTSIDE**.

I BELIEVE IN THOSE FORCES. I BELIEVE IN **DESTINY**. BUT I BELIEVE EVEN MORE IN **FREE WILL**. EVERYTHING WE DO, EVERY MOVE WE **MAKE**... ULTIMATELY, **THAT'S** WHAT DEFINES WHO WE ARE INSIDE...NOTHING **ELSE**.

YES, WE CAN BE **GUIDED** -- AS WE ATLANTEANS HAVE PLEDGED TO GUIDE **HUMANITY** --

-- BUT WHEREVER WE ARE, **WHOEVER** WE ARE, WE MEET OUR **ULTIMATE** FATE BECAUSE AND **ONLY** BECAUSE OF THE DECISIONS WE HAVE MADE AND MUST **LIVE** WITH.

THE ADMIRABLE...

...AND THE REGRETTABLE.

TIME IS A CIRCLE.

MAYBE NOT IN REALITY...BUT WITHIN THE CONFINES OF THIS GENERATOR, CERTAINLY.

THE SUPERCOLLIDER THAT SUPPLIES EARTH WITH ITS GRAVELECTRIC POWER CONTAINS FASTER-THAN-LIGHT TACHYONS...AND AS WE'VE SEEN, THAT TACHYON ENERGY TURNS THE TIMESTREAM INTO A WHIRLPOOL, PULLING IN ALL THOSE IT BRUSHES AGAINST...

...WHICH MEANS WE NEED TO FINISH REPAIRING THE COLLIDER WITHOUT LETTING THAT ENERGY TOUCH US.

I HAVE TO KEEP ONE EYE ON GALVAN. SINCE HIS BROTHER LEFT FOR PARTS UNKNOWN, HE'S BEEN UNDERSTANDABLY DISTRACTED.

THE OTHER EYE I KEEP ON THE UNCONSCIOUS PRISONERS WHO RUPTURED THE COLLIDER IN THE FIRST PLACE. BECAUSE OF THEM, VERITYN AND THE STRANGER WERE CAUGHT IN A WAVE OF CHRONAL ENERGY THAT SENT THEM...

NOR IS IT AS *SIMPLE* AS YOU SUGGEST. CONSIDER THIS:

THE ANOMALIES IN THE TIMESTREAM SURROUNDING AUSTRALIA WERE *UNIQUE* AND *LOCALIZED.*

THEY WERE *INFINITESIMAL* COMPARED TO WHAT YOU PROPOSE.

ALTERING THE OUTCOME OF *100,000 YEARS* IS STAGGERINGLY *DIFFERENT* AND STAGGERINGLY *DIFFICULT.* RIVERS DO NOT SIMPLY CHANGE *COURSE* WITHOUT AN *IMMENSE* DEAL OF *RESISTANCE.*

WE'D LIKELY FIND THAT THE TIMESTREAM WOULD *FIGHT* US AND IT...

...IT...

...SO MUCH TO *CONSIDER...* I'M WORRIED THAT I'M OVERLOOKING SOMETHING...

IS IT *SHOES?* YOU DIDN'T PACK ENOUGH *SHOES.*

THE *TRANSITION* ISN'T A *LAUGHING MATTER,* CAPRICIA.

WELL, NO *WONDER* YOU'RE SO INVESTED IN IT, THEN. HEY, WHEN YOU'RE ALL *ENLIGHTENED* AND EVERYTHING, DOES THAT COME WITH A SENSE OF *HUMOR?*

JOKE, DANIK. I'M *JOKING.*

YOU'RE STILL NOT CONVINCED I'M *GOING.*

I'M THINKING YOU'LL COME TO YOUR *SENSES,* YES. THE FUTURE IS *HERE,* DANIK, ON *EARTH* -- NOT IN PLAYING SOME COSMIC *LOTTERY* BY CREATING SOME SORT OF *GROUPMIND* IN THE *SKY.*

DON'T BE SO *IGN* --

"IGNORANT"? YOU WERE ABOUT TO CALL ME *IGNORANT?* I PUT UP WITH *THIS* FROM *YOU?*

AND I WOULD HAVE BEEN *WRONG.* I AM... I'M...

WHAT? *SORRY?* YOU DON'T HAVE TO *APOLOGIZE,* DANIK. I'M YOUR *FRIEND.*

YOUR *BEST* FRIEND. AND I JUST WANT THAT TO BE TRUE UNTIL WE'RE BOTH OLD AND *GRAY...*

HEL-*LO...?*

SO THE TIMESTREAM *FIGHTS* US. BIG *DEAL*.

YOU'RE POWERFUL ENOUGH TO FIGHT *BACK* AND FIGHT *THROUGH,* RIGHT?

WHAT?

OH. YES. YES, OF COURSE I AM. BUT THAT'S NOT THE *POINT.* THE *POINT* IS, WE *MUST* RETURN TO WHERE *WE* BELONG. THERE'S A *BIGGER PICTURE--*

YEAH! *YOU* DON'T GET TO BE A *GOD!* WHY DO YOU HAVE TO BE SO *SELFISH?*

VERITYN, IT ISN'T ABOUT--

YOU DON'T CARE ABOUT ANYBODY BUT *YOU? FINE! I'LL* TELL PEOPLE! *I'LL* WARN 'EM!

I'M GONNA SAVE MY *MOM* AND MY *DAD,* AND YOU CAN'T *STOP* ME! YOU *HEAR* ME?

YOU CAN'T *STOP* ME!

--AND THAT SHOULD ABOUT *DO* IT. HANG ON. IT'S NOT COMPLETELY *SEALED*, CAPRICIA.

BY *DESIGN*, GEROMI.

WE'RE NOT *FINISHED* HERE.

LEAVING SOME OF THE TEMPORAL ENERGY "LIVE" IS, ESSENTIALLY, OUR WAY OF LIGHTING A *BEACON* FOR VERITYN AND THE STRANGER.

I CAN'T SWEAR IT'LL DO ANY *GOOD*, BUT MAYBE IT'LL ESTABLISH A LINK OR A TETHER OF SOME SORT-- SOME *GUIDEPOST* FOR THEM.

EITHER WAY, WE'RE *NOT* ABANDONING *VERITYN*. GETTING HIM *BACK* IS OUR *ONLY* PRIORITY.

EVERYTHING *ELSE*, WE *IGNORE* FOR NOW.

DAD! DON'T *GO!* MOM, MAKE HIM *STAY!*

WE GOTTA MAKE EVERYBODY *STAY!*

VERITYN, VERITYN, W, AREN'T YO DRESSED FOR--

LISTEN TO ME!

THE *TRANSITION,* IT'S GONNA GO *WRONG* SOMEHOW AND WE'RE GONNA BE IN OUR *STASIS CHAMBERS* BUT WE WON'T BE *SAFE* WE'RE GONNA *SINK* ALL *ATLANTIS* IS GONNA SINK TO THE BOTTOM--

VERITYN...

--LISTEN! TO THE BOTTOM OF THE *OCEAN* AND WE'LL BE ASLEEP FOR A *HUNDRED THOUSAND YEARS* AND WHEN I WAKE *UP,* MOM, YOU'LL STILL BE *ASLEEP* BECAUSE HE CAN'T WAKE *YOU--*

WHO CAN'T--?

--AND THEN ALL THESE *MONSTERS* COME AFTER ME AND CAPRICIA AND THE *OTHERS* AND THEY'RE CALLED THE *NEGATION* AND THEY CUT CAPRICIA IN *TWO* AND THEY KILL EVERYBODY LEFT ON *EARTH* AND WE'RE ALL *ALONE* AND--

--AND--

SHHH. SHHH. IT'S *OKAY,* VERITYN. HUSH.

--AND YOU AND DAD ARE *GONE* AND--

SWEETHEART... *DARLING...*

...GO BACK TO *BED.*

YOU'RE HAVING A *BAD DREAM.*

WAIT. OKAY, *WAIT.* IF THEY SEE *TWO* OF US, THAT'LL PROVE--

NO.

YES! YOU *CAN* FIX ALL THIS, RIGHT? YOU *CAN!*

IF I SO *DESIRED,* YES. IT'S LIKELY I COULD EVEN PROTECT US FROM ANY RESULTANT *PARADOXES.* HOWEVER...

...

...HOWEVER, IT IS NOT...

...VERITYN, IT IS NOT OUR *PLACE* TO INTERFERE WITH *HISTORY*...!

"LOOK BELOW. LOOK *ABOVE*."

THE MOMENT OF TRANSITION IS *UPON* US, VERITYN. BASED ON WHAT I KNOW *NOW*, THE CAUSE OF THE *CATASTROPHE* BECOMES *APPARENT*.

WHEN WE PASSED THROUGH THE *DIMENSIONAL PORTAL* TO A NEW LEVEL OF *EXISTENCE*, WE OBVIOUSLY--*STUPIDLY*--*UNDERESTIMATED* THE RESULTING BACKLASH OF *ENERGY*.

THAT'S WHAT SANK ATLANTIS. THAT'S WHAT CRIPPLED THE AUTO-AWAKE MECHANISMS OF THE *STASIS TUBES* AND PLUNGED THOSE WHO *STAYED* INTO *ENDLESS SLUMBER*.

AND THAT IS WHAT WE WILL NOW PUT *RIGHT*.

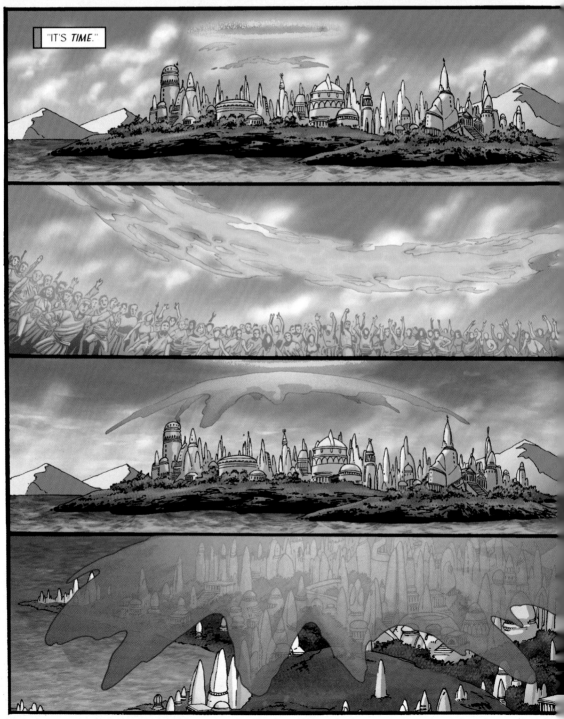

GO.

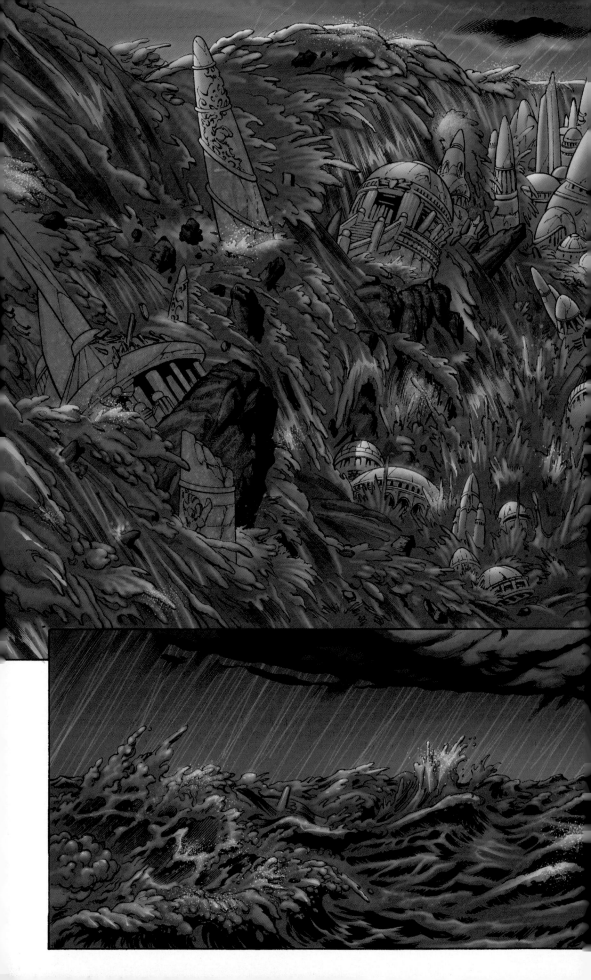

SO WHATEVER TUG AND THE OTHERS ARE UP TO, I'LL LEARN ABOUT *LATER*. RIGHT *NOW*, I'VE PULLED DANIK AND VERITYN ASIDE. THEY'VE BEEN KEEPING *SECRETS* FROM ME... *BIG* SECRETS...

...AND I'M ABOUT 100,000 YEARS *OVERDUE* FOR SOME *TRUTH*.

I ASSUMED THAT, BY NOW, YOU'D BE *ATTACKING* ME.

WAS THAT A *JOKE?* AREN'T *YOU* JUST FULL OF SURPRISES TODAY?

NO, *CLOCKING* YOU DIDN'T ACCOMPLISH ANYTHING *LAST* TIME. NOT THAT IT ISN'T *TEMPTING,* BUT BY NOW I THINK I'M JUST TOO *TIRED* TO GO THROUGH THAT AGAIN.

VERITYN-- YOU *KNEW* THIS, DIDN'T YOU? IF HE REALLY IS *DANIK,* WHY IN *CREATION* DID YOU *NOT* TELL US?

BECAUSE WE HAD A *PACT.* I *BARGAINED* FOR THE BOY'S *SILENCE.* WE MADE AN *EXCHANGE* THAT NEED NOT *CONCERN* YOU.

NEED NOT *CONCERN--?* YOU KNOW, I'M SUDDENLY FINDING MY *SECOND WIND. SAVE* US THE FIGHT AND JUST *EXPLAIN,* ALL RIGHT?

YOU WERE *THERE...TWICE!* WHAT *HAPPENED* TO SINK ATLANTIS? WHAT HAPPENED WITH *YOU?*

YEAH, YEAH. SEND THE *KID* AWAY.

AND IT'S JUST ABOUT TO GET REALLY *GOOD...*

VERY WELL.

THIS IS WHAT YOU *MISSED...*

NICE *ARMOR*. GOOD *FIT*. SEEMS A LITTLE *LOOSE* IN PLACES, THOUGH.

LET ME SEE IF I CAN TIGHTEN THAT *UP* FOR YOU A LITTLE BIT.

GGGNNNH!

K-KNCH

SEE, *TELEKINETICS* YOU DON'T WANT TO BE JERKING AROUND. *TALK*.

NOTHING? DO YOU HAVE ANY *CLUE* HOW SICK TO *DEATH* I AM OF *FIGHTING*? I'LL BE *FRANK*. IT DOESN'T COME *NATURALLY*.

I KNOW. BIG GUY LIKE *ME*... STILL, I WAS ALWAYS THE *BRAINY* ONE. NOT INCLINED TO SOLVE MY PROBLEMS WITH *DESTRUCTIVE ENERGY*.

I THREATEN YOU?

IN THE NEGATION HIERARCHY, I AM NOTHING. I AM LESS THAN THE WOOD-SPLINTER THAT JABS THE SKIN.

AND ONLY MY OWN OVERCONFIDENCE KEPT ME FROM SLAUGHTERING YOU.

ONLY DUMB LUCK SAVED YOU FROM BEING DESTROYED BY A SPLINTER.

AND I AM BACKED BY A FOREST.

YES, YOU AMUSE ME BECAUSE YOU SIMPLY CANNOT IMAGINE WHAT THE NEGATION IS...

...AND HOW MANY WAYS IT KNOWS TO KILL YOU ALL...

...STARTING, IF THERE IS ANY JUSTICE IN YOUR UNIVERSE AT ALL...

...WITH THAT ANNOYING BRAT CALLED VERITYN.

TUG, NO...

AND THAT EXPLAINS *THAT*. THAT'S WHY VERITYN SEEMS TO HAVE *CHANGED* SO MUCH SINCE WE *AWOKE*. HOW CAN SOMETHING LIKE THAT *NOT* FORCE HIM TO *GROW UP* A LITTLE?

MAYBE HIS "GLIMPSE" WAS SUPPOSED TO BE A GIFT, BUT IT'S ALSO A *BURDEN*...

...AND A BURDEN LIKE *THAT* IS TOUGH FOR *ANYONE* TO SHOULDER NO MATTER *HOW* OLD THEY ARE.

OH, DANIK...

YEP. 'COURSE, YOU KNOW WHAT I'M *TALKING* ABOUT, THOUGH...YOU BEING SUCH A *BIG PART* OF IT AND ALL.

...

WHAT?

HE DIDN'T...?

YOU GUYS TALKED SO LONG, I THOUGHT FOR *SURE* HE'D... *EXPLAIN* ABOUT...

ABOUT *WHAT*?

I REALLY DIDN'T SEE MUCH *MYSELF*...NOTHING THAT MADE *SENSE*, NOT RIGHT NOW... BUT CAPRICIA...

...I DON'T KNOW HOW, OR WHERE, OR WHEN... BUT SOMEDAY, YOU BECOME A *HUGE* PART OF THE MASTER PLAN.

A *HUGE* PART.

WHAT ARE YOU HOLDING *BACK*, DANIK?

WHY... WHY WOULDN'T HE TELL *ME* THAT?

'CAUSE IT'S A *BURDEN*, I GUESS.

WHY WOULD HE WANT TO PUT THAT *ON* YOU IF HE'S YOUR *FRIEND?*

WHY, INDEED...

with Steve Epting

CRITIX

Steve Epting has been a comics penciler for 13 years. He started his career with the now-defunct First Comics, drawing backup stories for NEXUS as well as various mini-series. After First folded, Steve penciled AVENGERS for several years and then a number of X-MEN titles for Marvel Comics before stints on SUPERMAN and AQUAMAN for DC.

Steve's work is distinguished by the expressiveness of his figures, his expert use of blacks, and a great sense of composition. His layouts lead your eye across the page effortlessly, and yet he rarely utilizes a simple grid to tell a story. Complex panel layouts are anchored by his deliberate use of black and a well thought out approach to placing figures on a page.

In this interview we talk to Steve about graphic design, visual storytelling, and the way the two interact on the comics page, then Steve takes us through all the steps that go into a single page from script to final.

Q. One thing that really stands out in your work is composition. Your layouts are dynamic, and even though there's a lot going on in your pages, it's very easy to follow.

A. Well I was a graphic design major in college, so I guess I want each page not only to work in a storytelling way but in a design sense. I look to have balance, readability, clarity, and composition — all the things that are involved in good graphic design. Those are the principles I try to apply to the visual look of a page as well as my storytelling.

Q. Yeah, your page layouts are extremely clear. I mean, you know where the eye is supposed to flow across the page.

A. I need to keep it clear, because I tend to use my

backgrounds a lot to define the page. If I'm not careful, the page can be too cluttered and the visual flow is interrupted.

Q. Many pages tend to have a single dominant panel anchoring them, visually and dramatically. They may not even be large or splashy panels, but there's almost always one panel that in a sense "organizes" the others. You may have five different panel shapes, but it reads as easily as a six panel grid.

A. I am using more simple layouts than I used to, but also more relatively small panels. Storytelling is very important to me, and that requires mixing it up.

During the big Image boom in the early '90s, editors were telling us all the opposite.

That's what the kids wanted: big panels with big impact. And the storytelling suffered. They would sort of wink at us and say, "Don't sacrifice storytelling, but…"

Q. And is that really a choice? Story vs. eye candy?

A. It's a matter of degree. You can't have an excessive quantity of big visual impact shots without storytelling suffering. A comic book has to work on two levels: visually or graphically (how the pages or panels look as pieces of art) and in terms of story-telling (how well they convey an idea). Structure is important to both sides of that.

Nick Cardy, one of my all time favorite comic artists, once compared comics storytelling to a symphony, where you have quiet moments that lead to crescendo. If you have no quiet moments, where's the crescendo? If you have 22 pages of in-your-face splash pages, then the splash has no impact. The splash should be used sparingly.

To put it another way, you need point and counterpoint to play off each other. If you have no lows, you have no highs.

Q. Now that works visually as well. Or I guess I should say "graphically," outside of the storytelling: the way you anchor images, spot blacks on the page, place figures in the panel. There's a strong component of contrast, of point-counterpoint within your pages.

A. Yeah. You're moving from close-ups to wider shots to create visual variety. If you have the same sized head in every panel you're just going to be bored looking at that. The same is true of full figure shots, even when they're in motion. You need variety in your shots, and you need to use that in furthering the storytelling.

But variety for variety's sake isn't everything. Nick told me once, "Say a person is walking into a house. You shoot them from an upstairs balcony. There's no reason for that down shot from the balcony unless you're going to establish that there's a character up there looking down."

There are other points of view. Joe Kubert is one of the best visual story-tellers, and he often uses a down shot for visual variety without a story reason for it. So it can be done and not kill a story. But Cardy is saying don't throw in camera angles just to be clever. There should be a reason you're doing what you're doing.

Q. Let's talk about your process. How do you begin to approach a page?

A. I read the script and, generally, there will be one panel that I will identify as the focus of the page (or of the two-page spread, as the case may be). Usually, I have the panel layout pretty much figured out in my head before I pick up a pencil. I might need to work out a thumbnail if it's an especially complicated sequence. A thumbnail is a sketch no more than a couple inches tall that's really useful for arranging objects on a page. You can whip them out pretty quick, so they give you the chance to work through a whole lot of different approaches quickly. I used to thumbnail everything, but after 12 years I'm pretty comfortable with what I come up with right away.

Anyway, the panel I've picked out will be the one that your eye is drawn to, the one with the most visual impact. It can be anywhere on the page, it can be any type of panel (an action shot, two people talking, whatever). Often the impact panel is one that I can envision working by itself, in isolation from the other panels.

Not every page will have one. That's part of the point-counterpoint. Some pages might have four horizontal panels in a grid, but then the next page would have an impact panel.

Q. You say the impact panel works 'by itself.' What do you mean?

A. In a sense every panel works by itself. But an impact panel has to work like a good painting — in that one image there's a story going on. Some panels, however, you may simply show a close up on a face or establish a setting. That's part of what Nick is talking about in comparing comics storytelling with a symphony.

This is the importance of the impact panel: No matter where it is on the page, your eye goes to the impact panel first, but that panel sends you back to the beginning. It's controlling the pace of your reading the page.

Q. Meanwhile, a panel is only an impact panel because you choose to make it one. What do you look for in an impact panel?

A. What's the most interesting image? Looking at the script for our sample page, the action explodes in panel two. You have a prelude, then the action panel, then repercussions that follow. So that presented itself to me as the logical point of impact.

This page follows a double page spread that establishes the characters in the scene and the setting, which is a mountain ridge overlooking an Aztec village. The current writer on CRUX, Chuck Dixon, writes 'full script,' which means I have the dialogue in hand before I start laying out the page. That helps when it comes to placing the figures within the panel, because you want their conversation to read left to right.

Anyway, let's take a look at this page.

In panel 1 Gannish and Yala are preparing for action. Zephyre and Verityn are just talking about what they're about to do.

Panel 2 is Gannish and Yala blazing away at these Aztec farmers. I've decided that this will be my impact panel.

Panel 3 Aztecs are falling under their bullets.

Panel 4 Zephyre and Verityn are confused.

Panel 5 Geromi explains the situation to Zephyre, which I've decided will be a close up.

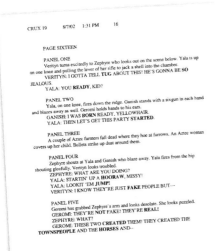

Q. You have a different process than most pencilers.

A. Yeah. Despite all the advanced color we have now, I tend to think very strongly in black and white. I tend to use a lot of solid blacks to balance the page. We sometimes call this 'spotting' blacks, because you're thinking about the blacks in terms of the page composition, not the figures or background as such.

Since that's my approach, I do fully-inked roughs before I actually begin penciling.

Q. For every page?

A. Yes, for every page. Of course they're inked with markers, and not with any finesse, but they are completely realized images with all the blacks filled in.

This is done on a piece of 8fi" x 11" paper that corresponds to the size of the final printed page. The reason I draw the rough this size is so that I can see exactly how it will work for the reader.

Everything is worked out on the rough, so that when I use a copier to enlarge it to 11" x 17" all the composition problems have been worked out. In that sense, the rough is where all the actual creative part takes place. There may be a little bit of tightening up when I place the expanded rough on a light box and start penciling the final page, but generally speaking the majority of the drawing takes place on the rough.

STEP ONE: BLOCKING THE PANELS

This is where the panels themselves take shape. I have a pretty good idea of the size and shape of each panel before I start blocking them in, but if something isn't working, this is where I make adjustments. That's why you want to keep things loose at this stage — you're adjusting for story and you're adjusting for composition.

I begin by blocking in panel placement and figures within the panel. I start placing figures in each panel, working from the foreground figures to the background figures. Since the foreground tends to be the focus, I like to work from foreground to background.

Once I'm comfortable with where the panels are placed, I'll ink in the borders around them before I begin the actual drawing. This defines the structure I'm working within and makes me more comfortable defining detail and thinking about balance.

Obviously, the details that come in first are in the figures, because that's the key focus of the story — the characters. So everything else is built around that.

STEP TWO: ESTABLISHING FOCUS

Once the figures are roughly blocked in, I'll go straight to pens and markers and work on the most important figure. In this case, it's Yala, who's in the foreground of the impact panel. I start in the foreground and work toward the background, concentrating on all the figures in the panel.

For this page, I draw the second panel all the way with pen and ink. I work one panel at a time, and this is the main panel. After the figures are in, then I know what the background needs to do.

For instance, on this page I know I need to be careful not to let the background compete with the figures. The background shouldn't compete. It's the setting, and it anchors the page.

In fact, because I've superimposed all the other panels "on top" of panel two, the heavy shadows on the left and right edge of the ridge help define the space without using a panel border. It creates a "wide-screen," open feeling, as if the setting extends beyond the page.

STEP THREE: FROM ROUGH TO PENCIL

I work one panel at a time, until the whole rough is done in pen and ink.
It remains rough, but the key elements are all there. I use a copier to
blow the rough up to 11" x 17", and place that on a light box. The light
box lets me see the rough clearly through the thick Bristol board I draw on.

On the penciled page you'll notice little "x" marks here and there. That's
a sign for Rick Magyar, the inker on CRUX, to place a flat black in the
whole area. There's no need for me to cover in pencil what he can do
better with ink and a brush.

STEP FOUR: FROM INKS TO COLOR

Rick is a great inker, and he puts a precise line on everything that I've drawn. When Rick is done with the page, everything is crisp and clear, and it's ready for Frank D'Armata to color.

Frank isn't just adding color, he's adding light and texture in a way that provides added depth to each panel. His color also distinguishes figures from the background and from each other in a way that can't be done in black and white, so you end up with a fully-realized world.

Yet everything is there from the rough. The layout is balanced, the impact panel draws the eye into the page and links the first and third panel, and there's a good interplay of light and dark. Roughing things out takes me 3-4 hours before I even set a pencil to the Bristol board, but for me there's no better way to get it right.

CROSSGEN COMICS

Graphic Novels

THE FIRST 1	Two Houses Divided	$19.95	1-931484-04-X
THE FIRST 2	Magnificent Tension	$19.95	1-931484-17-1
MYSTIC 1	Rite of Passage	$19.95	1-931484-00-7
MYSTIC 2	The Demon Queen	$19.95	1-931484-06-6
MYSTIC 3	Siege of Scales	$15.95	1-931484-24-4
MERIDIAN 1	Flying Solo	$19.95	1-931484-03-1
MERIDIAN 2	Going to Ground	$19.95	1-931484-09-0
MERIDIAN 3	Taking the Skies	$15.95	1-931484-21-X
SCION 1	Conflict of Conscience	$19.95	1-931484-02-3
SCION 2	Blood for Blood	$19.95	1-931484-08-2
SCION 3	Divided Loyalties	$15.95	1-931484-26-0
SIGIL 1	Mark of Power	$19.95	1-931484-01-5
SIGIL 2	The Marked Man	$19.95	1-931484-07-4
SIGIL 3	The Lizard God	$15.95	1-931484-28-7
CRUX 1	Atlantis Rising	$15.95	1-931484-14-7
NEGATION 1	Bohica!	$19.95	1-931484-30-9
SOJOURN 1	From the Ashes	$19.95	1-931484-15-5
SOJOURN 2	The Dragon's Tale	$15.95	1-931484-34-1
RUSE 1	Enter the Detective	$15.95	1-931484-19-8
THE PATH 1	Crisis of Faith	$19.95	1-931484-32-5
CROSSGEN ILLUSTRATED Volume 1		$24.95	1-931484-05-8